MONTI'S STORY

MONTI'S STORY
Love Lifted Me

Second Edition

Trish Harleston

with compiled writings by Monti F. Finnie

TATE PUBLISHING
AND ENTERPRISES, LLC

Published by Tate Publishing & Enterprises, LLC
127 E. Trade Center Terrace | Mustang, Oklahoma 73064 USA
1.888.361.9473 | www.tatepublishing.com

Tate Publishing is committed to excellence in the publishing industry. The company reflects the philosophy established by the founders, based on Psalm 68:11,
"The Lord gave the word and great was the company of those who published it."

Cover Photo by Evin Grant, by Grantphotography
Cover Concept by Tanesha Rowe
Cover design by Eileen Cueno
Interior design by Jomel Pepito

Published in the United States of America

ISBN: 978-1-63367-580-3
Family and Relationships
14.10.10

Dedication

"This is dedicated to my late mother, Deloris R. Finnie, as she was granted the miracle of being able to give birth. God created my life and my mother gave birth to it. Upon being conceived, my mother began immediately leading me on the right path. All a part of God's Great Plan.

I would first like to thank my Heavenly Father God for giving me the "Gifts" to write this material and for His unchanging Love. Without Him nothing is possible. I would also like to thank my Best Friend, Anita K. Harris, who has been a constant and genuine love in my life, as well as a trusted confidant. Another part of God's Plan. I can't forget my Big Brother, Joseph A. Finnie, who has always been an umbrella that has sheltered me from harm while we were growing up, and even now, he still looks out for me. My brother and I are as different as night and day, and for that reason I didn't always know how much my "big bro" actually loved me. Not only do I know it now, but I realize just how much he always has.

Finally, I'd like to thank my family who have always been there, as well as believed in my abilities. And thanks so much to the readers whose support and inspiration have urged me to write this material. I pray that all who are recognized here and anyone who reads this literature, gets as much out of reading it as I did from writing it."

Monti Finnie

This book is dedicated to the memory of Monti Fitzgerald Finnie and to my family. No matter what any of us were going through, you always allow us to do so privately, while providing unwavering love and support.

Trish Harleston

ACKNOWLEDGEMENTS

Thank you Lord for favor!

Thank you to the best husband in all the earth. He is the one who treats me as his queen, who has supported my many paths, projects and whims over the years. You have applauded me, prayed for me and always reminded me that I was not traveling this road alone.

Thank you to my children, Nikki and Evin, two young people who deserve the whole world, yet have always been absolutely pleased with having just me.

Thank you, T.Rowe for being the creative genius who brings my vision to life.

Thank you to my friends for your love and support. Special thanks to Reka and Lysa for holding me accountable to my commitment to finish this book.

Thank you to my mother who shows me that she's proud of the woman I have become and of what God is doing in my life.

Thank you to my brothers, sisters, nieces and nephews for making this a family project. Thanks to each of you for reading the manuscript, for being my backbone, and for allowing conversation on this difficult topic.

Thank you to Beverly, the Diva Author, for being the one who motivated me to keep writing after I had put this story down. Thank you for inspiring and encouraging me to create a book that others would want to read.

Finally, thank you to my Pastor and my Orange Grove family. Thank you for making room for my gifts at OG and for allowing me to bloom.

But the Master of the sea, heard my despairing cry,
from the waters lifted me, now safe am I.

Love lifted me,
Love lifted me.

When nothing else would help,
Love lifted me.

Words from the Hymn "Love Lifted Me"
James Rowe, 1912

CONTENTS

Introduction

"Prepare to be moved and inspired."

—*Monti*

Several years have passed since the death of my nephew, Monti Finnie, and I am finally led to share his story—in his words. His life was one that was filled with far too many years of grief and depression, a period that he referred to as "darkness". Once he found Jesus, he had no stronger desire than to be with Him; yet, he continued to regularly sink into this place of desperation and despair. This behavior was perceived as somewhat strange to those who knew him because this desire for divine closeness manifested itself in ways that were often misunderstood. Because of an overwhelming frustration associated with being misinterpreted or misrepresented, he would often retreat to a place that seemed distant to some. It was in this place where I believe he did much of his writing. It was also this place where his desire to be with the Father was stronger than his desire to remain on this earth. The desire was so strong, that it may have contributed to his neglecting the reality of the life that he was destined to live on earth, and caused him to often disconnect from those who cared for him so deeply. Of all the people I know, Monti was the one person whom I believe truly felt like a foreigner in this land and who knew that the only true peace he would ever have was with his Savior. God's Word says that we are in this world, but are not of this world. As I spent time reading his writings and exploring what were probably his innermost thoughts, I came to realize that even when he tried with everything that was within him, he could not seem to find that place of refuge we are promised when we find Jesus. He longed for a much deeper love and a much deeper relationship than could be found in humanness. He longed for a connection of spirits that would only be revealed when the spirit is no longer housed in flesh. Therefore, I believe that he found it difficult to live in this world when all he ever really wanted was to live with Jesus.

What was incredibly amazing about his life is that he fought tirelessly to unravel what was going on in his mind and in his heart. Even though it kept him hostage for years, he never stopped searching for the light that he knew had to be out there. I believe that he genuinely knew what it was to love unconditionally, but I'm not sure that he ever really understood what it meant to receive love from others.

My prayer is that God will allow me to successfully and accurately narrate his writings and capture his thoughts. And, from the memory of our lengthy conversations, I hope to portray his life in the manner in which he would have wanted it communicated.

Rev. Trish Harleston
Aunt of Monti Finnie

(All drawings and italicized writings throughout this book, unless otherwise noted, were Monti's original work.)

"BUT I AM DESTINED FOR ANOTHER LAND—MY HOMELAND—THIS PLACE IS FOREIGN."

MONTI

CHAPTER 1

Have pity upon me, have pity upon me, O ye my friends;
for the hand of God hath touched me. Job 19:21

TOUCHED BY GOD

"How do I know God is real? I've been touched. How do I know Jesus redeems? I've been touched. How do I know the Holy Spirit fills? I've been touched." This statement, taken from a sermon by William D. Watley on Facing the Untouchable[1], was highlighted in a book by the same author. The book entitled, *You Have to Face It to Fix It* was one of many in which Monti took the liberty to insert his personal thoughts.

Beneath Pastor Watley's message was Monti's handwritten note:

...THANK YOU, OH LORD FOR YOUR TOUCH...

---

1. William D Watley, "Facing the Untouchable." *You Have to Face It to Fix It*: Judson Press, 1997, (81)

Many of Monti's writings were assembled together in storybook format which he had included a cover page with a story title that simple stated *"Thank You"* in bold letters on the front. The introduction for this story that contained some of the most personal and intimate details of his life, consisted of four lengthy paragraphs simply thanking God for his existence.

For most of us, it takes nearly a lifetime to realize that we were created to offer worship and thanksgiving unto God. Because we search for substitutes to fill the void when this relationship is absent, we spend an enormous amount of time trying to find fulfillment in life. We are created for God's glory, therefore, we are unfulfilled until we are living a life that brings glory and honor to Him. Genuine fulfillment is not found through accumulation, but in release. Accumulation of things can distract us from the true purpose and destiny for which God has set before us.

An amazing revelation is that we serve a God who gives us much, who loves us much and who actually requires very little. Think about it, we have made this simplistic reality more complex than it is. Monti understood and was drawn in by the promise of this reality. We have been convinced that God requires much from us. On the surface that appears to be the case. But, in addition to obeying His Word He requires three basic things from His children. He requires that we "**be** holy, because He is holy," that we "**seek** first His kingdom and righteousness," and that we "**confess** our sins." These requirements demand that we address three areas of our life that we often avoid. <u>To be</u> holy requires a change in behavior and often a change in attitude. <u>To seek first</u> requires a change in priorities and a change in time management. <u>To confess</u> requires that we first acknowledge; therefore it requires a degree of self-evaluation.

But, Monti must have realized in his short span of thirty seven years that we can only please God when we make no concern about pleasing others or self. Personal pleasure is simply satisfaction for the flesh and we know that anything that pleases the flesh is temporal. Therefore, the touch that our hearts long for is an eternal satisfaction that comes only when the flesh is denied.

God requires that we seek intimacy with Him as a priority in life. Non-believers don't completely understand why this has to be the primary relationship in our lives. However, when we set this truth as the foundation for why we exist, that is when fulfillment is realized and when the answers to the complex questions of life are revealed.

Monti's story is a simple story of truly seeking God with his whole heart. It is his journey of searching for the light that would draw him out of his darkness. He gives us insight into how he gained understanding of loving God in the way that we were designed to love God. In his last days, I believe that he may have made a decision to somehow neglect his love for life in an effort to find the place where he might satisfy his longing for a deeper place with Jesus.

Even though we are commanded to deny ourselves as part of our spiritual walk toward following Christ, the reality is that denying self and neglecting life are not synonymous.

...for He is why I exist—Why we all exist. I owe all that I am to Him. Occurrences throughout my past, the good as well as the bad, have all developed me into who I am at the present...and although I very recently became "saved," these occurrences have brought me to the level of spirituality and to the relationship with God that I now possess. I have spent too many years of my life, nearly 30 years, not giving the appreciation to my Lord nor giving Him the recognition He deserves for loving me, for giving me sweet mercy and for so many wonderful blessings during my entire life. To some degree, I guess I was taking for granted all that God had done for me. I was finally ready to look to God for help. And though He had been there all along, a new life was created in me and a wonderful journey was embarked upon in the name of the Lord. He restored "Hope" for the "Blessings" and "Salvation" which was right there waiting for me to ask, and He renewed in me the wonderful plan He has prepared for my "Future."

I now have a new appreciation and spirit of expectancy for God's Plan. I also have a greater understanding of the Love that is God. He is now my Alpha and Omega—my beginning and my end, because His love has become personal in my life. I can finally see how everything did indeed work together for my good; and I trust in Him, that all things...always will. In the name of Jesus, I Pray—Amen.

Monti

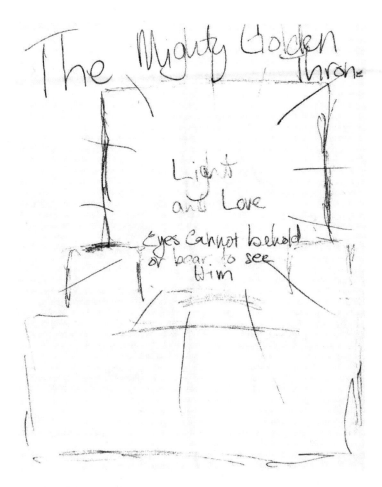

The Mighty Golden Throne—Light and Love
Eyes cannot behold or bear to see Him.

CHAPTER 2

"Henceforth I call you not servants; for the servant knoweth not what his lord doeth: but I have called you friends; for all things that I have heard of my Father I have made known unto you." John 15:15

THE TASK OF LOVING YOURSELF

We can learn a lot about a person by reading their journal. Although I wouldn't recommend it without permission, reading the pages of a journal gives insight into the innermost thoughts and into the deepest desires and dreams of the writer. As a journaler, I can say that because we never think that anyone else will dare to unlock these pages of our life, we can freely use them to pour out our heart and soul.

Most of the insertions in Monti's journal read as short conversations with God. They are not deep and revelatory dialogue, but quick "check-in" moments with a good friend. Through these noted journal entries, it is easy to see that this year was a particularly transitional year for Monti. But through it all, it's easy to see the depth of God's love in his heart. He often wrote of how he loved everyone. But even more, it's easy to see through his writings that he loved the Lord. However, it seems that the task of loving himself may have been one of his greatest challenges. The agony of losing his mother—the period he describes as despair—had a greater impact on how he felt about himself than I think any of us ever realized.

I am grateful for many things. As I looked closely at Monti's life, I am grateful that He knew that he was loved. I am grateful that he knew others were praying for him. But most of all, I am grateful that he knew the Lord in the midst of his despair and agony—in the midst of his darkness, he found how to search for the light.

From Monti's Journal:

February 15, 2002

Father God, Lord Jesus, It's true, I don't claim to know what the big picture is—my purpose, my future, my destiny. I do know that I want to do your will, Oh Lord. I know that I am the righteousness of God and I intend to remain with that assurance. It is by the blood of Jesus Christ that I am saved and given this wonderful gift of salvation. Only you know everything and I rejoice and trust in that. Amen.

FEBRUARY 22, 2002

Lord Jesus, Father God and the Holy Ghost

I say thank you O Lord. When I lost my mother in 1992, I was in shock. Then I buried my despair and thought I'd leave it behind in Massachusetts where my mom passed away. My job was closing so I moved to Florida to keep my job with AT&T in 1993. From 1993 'til approximately 1996 or 1997, I tried to get lost in the club scene and friends (supposedly), but I had to deal with my despair and what it was doing to my life. Then "You" stepped into my life and I was delivered from the despair and found a new hope and positive outlook toward my future. It made me strong in that I gained independence and reliance upon only you and no person here on earth. Thank you Lord for releasing my mother from her suffering. Thank you for your mercy and your saving grace and your blessings and miracles, your sacrifices and sweet salvation.

FEBRUARY 28, 2002

Father God, Lord Jesus and the Holy Ghost, I am reaching to you to help me. Please restore my peace and my joy. I have put forth the effort but it has left me chained. I need to be put back on the right path. I need your radiant light. Please Lord, restore your grace and guide me on the way I should go or else just handle this current dilemma that is troubling me. I know I need to let it go and let God. But I can't seem to shake it. I am sorry O Lord that I am not stronger or that I can't switch courses with greater speed but I want to be more at peace with myself. Please help me O Lord.

MARCH 4, 2002

I have never been fired from a job and I have worked at this same job since August 1990 (Thank you Lord). But right now, I feel like getting fired is the way to move into the occupation God has in store for me. I will keep my eyes, spirit and my heart open so I can see when the Lord leads me elsewhere. Until then, thank you Lord.

MARCH 8, 2002

There is nothing that is beyond God's power. I confess that I was once dealing with trying to control my rage. I had a cat that became unruly after a time and I found myself over disciplining him…yes…I was abusing my defenseless little cat. He was completely defenseless against me, a big human man! I gave the cat away to save him, as well as to save myself. The Lord still loves me so I know I'm okay—but I am so sorry I did it. It tore me up inside. But I had to face that I was the victimizer. I have repented.

MARCH 18, 2002

Father God Lord Jesus and the Holy Ghost…I thank you Lord for the many years you have blessed me at this job. It has its perks and benefits and has great pay. It has been great to me and I am truly grateful. But after 12 years, they announced they will be laying off our entire building. May 12th is my final day of active employment. Though my future is unknown, I will remain faithful to you. Even so, my thought right now is of peace, comfort and a positive outlook for my future. I am saved 3 years now. My faith is strong. My spirituality has grown. I have felt directed to go home (North Carolina / Virginia) and I will finally be on my way in a couple of months. I do and will continue to pray that You, O Lord, will lead the way and will keep me. Where you lead me Lord, I shall follow. I have you. I love everyone and I love me. Thank you. I praise you and glorify you, Your child always, Monti.

April 11, 2002

Lord Jesus, Father God and Holy Spirit, it was officially announced. Our office will be closing on May 14, 2002. Finally after almost 12 years, Lord, you have delivered me to a better place. I am going to share in spiritual love with my family and with new and some old friends. I will not fear anything, Lord. I will believe and keep the faith that you will be watching, protecting, and continuing to bless me. I am tempted by lust though I have learned to suppress my actions with your wonderful deliverance. Also my crutch continues to call me. Please help me to turn away from those habits. They only hold me back. I want to be a writer to use this precious gift you gave me O lord. I pray to do your will. *{Bold* *emphasis added} However you see fit, Lord, deliver me from the temptations I was exposed to in Jacksonville. I've outgrown my old life and my old ways. I pray for my best friend, I pray for my co-workers, all of my friends and Lord, I pray for everybody. I love everyone!*

MAY 16, 2002

Father God, Lord Jesus, and Holy Ghost, I humbly pour out to you. My life is truly blessed. I know this because I know YOU and I am grateful for all that you do. I was able to pay my rent just in time. This is the last full month at this address after over nine years. More blessings, as well as bigger and better blessings await me as my (your) journey takes me to North Carolina. I am expecting my money to arrive between May 24 and 31. Having that will be a break in my monetary worry or concern. (A sigh of relief) Thank you! Here I am at the edge, so close to God's great and awesome wonder…watching the beach, the waves are breaking on the shore. Water is always moving. It's so loud, yet it's soothing, soft and deep. I am amazed at you Lord! You are my everything. Some people can't understand my contentment and my faith under these circumstances. But I am so grateful that I feel your peace. I am comforted by your presence and your existence in my life. I know you will provide, and I know that everything will be fine. As your word states, you will take care of me and my needs. I trust in you. I love you. I thank you O Lord. If you lead me, I will follow. Draw me toward my calling, purpose, and my duty...I pray, in Jesus name, Amen.

JULY 1, 2002

Lord Jesus, Holy Ghost and most of all, Father God, I am finally feeling the challenges of losing my job in May. I prayed about where to go and I know that You showed me the way. I'm in North Carolina with all the people I love...I'm with my family. I love everyone, with the love of Christ. I didn't hesitate to move and I have faith in you. O Lord I know that you can move mountains, I need a barber here, please help me find one that I'm ok with. I'm here with my grandma whom I love so much. She is the love and strength and the cornerstone of this family. Lord, I need a new job, and I know, O Lord that you will make it happen. Please direct me O Lord for when I should make the next move, or if I should move. I thank you and love you and I trust in you, O Lord, Amen.

JULY 31, 2002

Father God, Lord Jesus and Holy Ghost, It's ironic that this particular story came up today. I have a friend who has been in the darkness of misery for 8 years or so because she was in a relationship where a man treated her very badly. I wasn't there nor is it my life, but there is so much pain from what she feels like he did to her, there is so much depression. Dear Lord, I have talked, yelled, and cried to her and for her. Nothing seems to work, she doesn't know what to do. I don't know what to do for her. It's not my place or responsibility to try to change other people or their situation. I can do what I can to encourage and inspire them, but people have to ask of the Lord themselves for help for only He can do all things. I have sent her my book and I hope that my testimony might help in some way. I have expressed love and gratitude of our friendship. The rest is up to her. Please Lord touch her heart. I pray that things will turn around.

August 24, 2002

Father God, Lord Jesus and Holy Ghost, I would first like to thank you for everything. When I lost my mother, it was really hard for me. I went through a despair that would span almost a decade, but Lord you were there with me and brought me through one trial after another. I looked away from you and caused many of these trials to come into my fragile life. When I finally gave my life to you, O Lord, it was right on time. I had wasted so much of my life—so many years. But I can say that I learned a lot. But in May of 1999, I found a relationship with you and it has been the most wonderful thing that has ever happened in my life. It will be you, Lord, for the rest of my life. So, for as long as you see fit Lord, I will follow you! I am grateful and I am blessed. I am a child of God and I will forever stay focused on you, O Lord. Please keep me in your good and saving grace just as you always have. Do it Lord until I see you face to face. Please forgive me for all of my sins. I love you Lord…Thank you for loving me. These things I pray in the name of Jesus, Always.

Monti

Note: No further entries were made in this journal.

CHAPTER 3

"Casting all your care upon him; for he cares for you."
I Peter 5:7

REACHING BACK

Regardless of what circumstances we face in adulthood, many of us still have fond memories of our childhood. Monti's childhood was no different. My sister did everything within her natural power and financial ability to ensure that her two young boys didn't feel the impact of what most kids felt from living in a single parent household. They were not going to be emotionally affected by having to live on welfare or in subsidized housing. She was determined to accomplish this, not through showering them with gifts, but through sharing a love of family unlike what I have seen in many young mothers.

It was obvious to everyone who knew them that these two young men greatly

respected the woman whom they always so affectionately called "Mah." This was a woman who exhibited a powerful, dominating personality that was much greater than the appearance of her small-framed stature. She displayed a strength that was threatening to anyone who dared to mistreat her sons. She absolutely did not tolerate any misuse of authority in any institution toward her boys; they were going to always receive fair and equitable treatment. Everyone in the neighborhood, in their circles and in the streets of their city, knew that this petite woman, who stood less than five feet tall, was a force to be reckoned, and no one dare underestimate her.

Monti's childish laughter and boyish smile that was so infectious and usually present when his mother was near became silenced at her death. I don't know if there was ever a moment following her death when he was truly able to reach back to find that place of genuine joy.

Reach back with me…Reach…deeper…further…reach. As the haze begins to clear, I can see an image becoming clearer and clearer. I can hear faint laughter, overlapping laughter. It's the sound of children playing and laughing. It's a birthday party. Is it my brother's birthday? Is it my birthday? Not quite sure as our birthdays are just days apart, and many times, were celebrated on the same day.

There I am, standing against the wall. But the laughter taking place is not mine. I am pouting, which was not unusual for me. I must have been five years old at that time and in the eyes of those who loved me, I was still a baby.

In my recollection, this was typical of my childhood—a party; life taking place all around me—and me on the outside, looking in and pouting. I don't know why but I never felt much like a part of the many celebrations that occurred around me. Perhaps it was because of family and life changes that were presented when I was young. Maybe I never really understood what was going on around me. Or maybe I understood but just never came to grips with the changes. The breakup and eventual divorce of my parents, or the move from my familiar surroundings to Massachusetts—these were lifestyle changes that occurred when I was a child that had a huge effect on me. I believe that these changes created uneasiness about my future that remained with me for years.

I feel like my mother became a single parent by choice; she chose not to stay married. I never understood how she was able to do it. How was it that she was always able to provide love, security, and discipline with strength, independence and determination in a bodily frame that that was so much smaller than my brother and me? She was a small woman whose giant spirit and strong influence allowed her to give all she had, which was all we really needed. It is still unclear whether this was her way of ensuring that we would have minimal impact associated with the lack of our father in our lives. Or maybe this was her way of proving to everyone that she didn't need a man to successfully raise two men. I don't know how or why, but what I do know is that by God's grace, our needs were always met.

The early seventies was a time of peace and love and happiness. Many of the songs and movies during this era were influenced by this period of seemingly peace. Some of the images I remember in our household during that time were the large silver can of peanut butter with the oil floating on top or the long block of cheese, and I remember the necessity of controlled or subsidized rent. This image symbolized welfare dependency, yet, we didn't realize that we were dependent because we had not a care in the world. This was our world. It was the world we knew so it was perfect in our eyes. We were always able to live in pleasant neighborhoods with lots of other kids to play with. It felt like the sun shone directly on our home all the time, even when there was snow on the ground. Pastel colored brick buildings and green grass; this was our neighborhood.

I will always cherish the memory of the great strides to which my mother went to teach us self-worth. She taught us never to look down on anyone and she made sure that we understood our value and would let no one look down on us. Material things did not determine our value. I loved hearing my mother tell us that we were special. Of course all mothers tell their children that, right? But I believed that if she said it, it had to be true. I now understand that special didn't mean that we were better, because she wasn't using it to make comparisons. It was simply her way of reminding us that we were created in the image of God, and therefore, no one had the right to downplay that image in us!

One of my fondest memories of childhood was time spent at the Boys and Girls Club. At that time, I didn't realize the impact that organization would have on my development as a young man. It afforded me the opportunity to associate with different cultures and children of different ages who were all there for the same reason…because there would be no parent at *home when we got out of school. What I remember most about the club was that it was a place that had everything for kids… There were playgrounds, pools, basketball courts, table tennis. We would do talent shows, have cooking classes, and do arts and crafts. I believed that there was no better place for a child when I was growing up. It was a constructive place with a positive influence.*

My mother made sure that our lives were sheltered from many of the heartbreaking realities that seemed to be a part of the reality of many youth in single parent, urban homes. Later, we would hear stories of child molestation, child abandonment, child abuse and the like. My mother's life was spent making sure that our lives were free of these cares. I think it is this foundation on which I am now able to stand with confidence and with love of family. She made sure that we knew the difference between right and wrong choices, good and bad groups. Sometimes the lessons were tough but she made sure that we knew the consequences of decisions made. As a young boy, my perception of my mother was one of perfection in my innocent, young eyes. However, it would be years before I would realize just how mortal and imperfect she was. She made us feel that she would always be there to bear our burdens. It was perhaps for this reason, that we didn't understand that it was God who we would ultimately need to carry us and to carry the weight. She instilled in us that we could overcome anything if we were strong enough. But what we didn't know was that it was in our weakness that Christ is made strong in us, so we didn't have to worry about being strong enough, if we simply knew how to trust God. We were taught many lessons growing up in that single parent household, but the one thing that was missing was conversation about the importance of a relationship with God. We would sometimes go to church, and of course we heard about God from time to time. We had seen pictures of Jesus hanging on the wall in many homes. Therefore, we had a visual of what we thought he "looked like"; we didn't know that it was critical that we actually get to know HIM. We missed an important message about the magnificent and very personal relationship that He wanted to have with us. That would only prove to be important when my mother died and left us "seemingly alone."

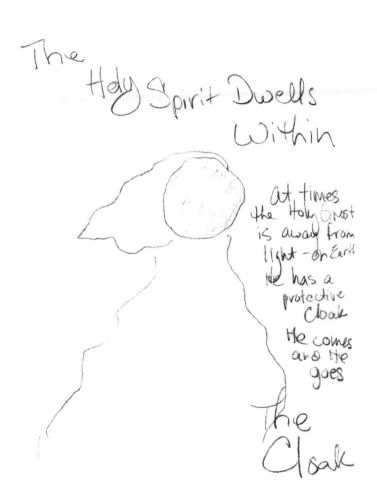

The Holy Spirit Dwells Within
At times, the Holy Ghost is away from light–on earth
He has a protective cloak–He comes and He goes
The Cloak

CHAPTER 4

"Fear thou not; for I {am} with thee: be not dismayed;
for I {am} thy God: I will strengthen thee; yea, I will
help thee; yea, I will uphold thee with the right hand of
my righteousness." Isaiah 41:10

NOW COMES THE DRAMA

Isn't it interesting that those things that seemed incredibly important as a teenager are a tiny blur of a memory today? The drama for many us during those teenage years consisted of a pimple the size of a mustard seed that felt like a watermelon on our face. Yet, for others it was the agony of not getting asked out by the only one true love in life that we think will ever exist for us. In either case, as a teenager, we just didn't know how we would ever survive the trials and the drama that we had to endure.

Whether it's the 70s, the 80s, or the new millennium, young drama will inevitably

involve adolescent sexuality and hormonal confusion. There is a place in the cycle of life called puberty. I define it as the place where God perhaps took His break, and when he returned, forgot where he left off. He obviously left this phase in a young person's life unfinished. This can't be on purpose, this place of being stuck between childhood and adulthood in the physical body yet, not allowing the mental state to operate on the same timetable.

I remember much about these years in Monti's life, for it was the time when I moved from North Carolina to Massachusetts and spent a few months sharing space in their two-bedroom apartment. For some reason, my oldest nephew didn't seem to suffer the same physical challenges as a pre-teen that Monti was dealing with. Some young people survive those years with what appears to be minimal changes, and then others deal with such traumatic changes in appearance that they would love to go into hiding until that period passes.

After I moved out, Monti spent enormous amounts of time at our home; he and my daughter developed a relationship much like that of a brother and sister. He would often spend the night, playing with her and her friends. But when he got older, he didn't want to be bothered with them. Not long after that, he went off to college. We would sometimes drop him off at school as though we were his proud parents.

Back to the phase that he called drama…Emotionally, he seemed to be enjoying this period. He seemed to have many friends, he was quite smart in school, but he was still very much his momma's baby boy. As I reflect on this period, I remember a happy boy who seemed to have no interest in sexual intimacy. He didn't talk much about girlfriends or relationships. So it came as quite a surprise to read that much of what was documented about this time period was sexually influenced. Could it be that adolescent boys, are sexually curious yet emotionally confused? Although they are processing through physical maturation, they still lack understanding regarding the changes in their young bodies? Perhaps as an adult looking back on those years, Monti only remembered how his present life was so greatly influenced by what was happening at that time?

Being a teenager in the eighties brought a new word to my vocabulary...drama! Many people remember the eighties as a time for disco and funky beats. Others remember the eighties as a time of war and violence, domestically and abroad. It was a time of increasing numbers in gang wars, and drugs becoming more visible in a city where we had once found so much peace. I also remember it as a time when a new word was introduced that would forever change how the world viewed sexuality... AIDS!

In the early to mid 80s, there was a lot of talk about sexual partners, about being more aware and selective about who you had sex with. Everybody was concerned with the number of sexual partners and how easy it was to become affected and infected. It was a scary time and we didn't really understand it...all we knew was that anything that involved exchange of bodily fluids was under scrutiny. We were scared to go to public bathrooms, afraid to use the silverware in restaurants for fear of contamination. And we were told to make sure not to touch anyone who looked sick. There was so much fear associated with this unknown disease. But the greatest fear surrounding this disease, and understandably so, was that it was so lethal that it not only would inevitably end in death, but it would cause a social death of sorts that would precede the actual physical death. It was fear along with ignorance that would cause people to think twice before leaping into a sexual relationship. A few minutes of pleasure could cause a lifetime of pain. But then, we were just kids, so none of his would apply to us.

But what I later found out was that it was during this time that many of the young people my age were boasting about losing their virginity. Believe it or not, it was not uncommon to hear of someone as young as 12 becoming sexually involved. Most of the kids I knew had already experienced sex before even turning 16. Let me take a moment and smile as I reflect on my first time. It was surprisingly pleasant, quite memorable and with someone whom I cared a lot about at that time. I didn't feel like we were confused young teenagers and we didn't worry about what this would mean later. Though, this was a pleasant experience, I wish that I would have waited. In retrospect, I wish that I could say that I was a virgin until marriage. Oh well, since I'm still not married, and I'm obviously no virgin, that's the end of that wishful thought.

If I had the opportunity to speak to every young person that I know, I would tell them to make every effort to WAIT. Whatever it takes, "Just say no," "Turn around and walk away," "Cross your legs," "Take a cold shower," or "run a marathon!" Because *the truth is that once you've crossed that bridge, and you know what's on the other side, your flesh wants to keep crossing that bridge as much as you can make your way across it. Once the flesh gets a taste of the feeling, it makes any thought of future living as saved and celibate so much more difficult. Most of the time, it's easier to give in and just backslide. But let me take a minute and return to my holiness posture…because even writing it about it brings up some unholy thoughts…so, Lord, give me strength.*

Many of those years as a teenager are a blur in my mind today. Perhaps it is because that was such a difficult time in my life that I've subconsciously blocked it out. These were indeed some of the hardest years of my young life. During most of the years between twelve and sixteen I was trying to figure out who this person was that God placed inside my body. This is the time in the life of most teenagers when all we want is to be popular. We will do everything necessary not to be outcast from the normal, popular kidsThis is when I recall my first exposure to my personal drama. I've battled with skin problems and severe acne for most of my life. Although it has improved a great deal in recent years, I have not resolved internally that this look might be my permanent fate. For a young person, there is not much worse than feeling like you look awkward. I remember wishing for physical changes more than for anything else in the world. It's amazing that even as an adolescent somehow I knew that the physical challenges I struggled with today would not compare to the psychological challenges I would face in the years ahead.

As a teenager, I felt that I was mature beyond my years. Therefore it was no surprise that I could endured the many ups and downs, struggles and triumphs, good days and bad which came my way. Even with this pre-mature maturity that I felt I had, I still faced much of this with my eyes wide shut, either voluntary or involuntary. But mine were no different than most adult struggles, the decision between worldliness and Godliness. So, what constituted the drama…? The drama was primarily the result of trying to deal with raging hormones, acting grown before adulthood, and then of course, becoming exposed to sex far too soon.

To a young man with severe acne and self-esteem issues, almost everything about growing up created a new level of drama. No looking the way I thought I should look, not feeling the way I thought I should feel, not dressing the way I wanted to dress—all created drama in my mind. My mom was a price-conscious shopper (actually, economics required her to be). I was always neat and clean and my clothes were always appropriate, but I would not have won any best-dressed awards among my friends. I never looked as good as I thought I should look, because even at that time, clothes and appearance were important to me. So here I was, desiring to look grown up, yet, mom just kept saying to me was to stop trying to grow up so fast. With my "yeah, I already know everything" attitude, I would respond "yep, I hear you." More drama—I felt that my look on the outside didn't accurately reflect the person I thought I was from the inside. As I think upon the changes the body goes through from childhood to adulthood, I realize that the physical changes don't compare to the psychological changes that occur while maturing through adolescence. There has to come a time when we either slow down or catch up with wherever we are supposed to be as a young person. I would often wonder if I was at the right place at the right time. I now know that was all a part of that phase of growing up, and every phase is short-lived. But I thank God for peace and for giving me the assurance that at just the right time, I will receive all of the precious gifts that God is waiting for me to claim and unwrap.

This chapter makes me smile, because even as Monti spent time obviously reminiscing about the years he described as drama, he apparently paused to think about where he was and the level of peace he had deep within.

I sincerely thank God for growth, especially Spiritual growth. How ironic that now, with my twenties completely behind me forever, that at the start of this new Millennium, my journey on life's path is truly just beginning. I now feel a peace that is breathtaking, and a love that is reassuring, comforting, and unconditionally never-ending. These things I have searched for all my life…

Yet to now know that my Father was there all along… I breathe!

CHAPTER 5

"Blessed {are} they that mourn: for they shall be comforted." Matthew 5: 4

THE DARKNESS SETS IN

THE REAL WORLD—

REALITY—

WHAT IS THAT?

Why does everyone think I'm not facing reality? Why do I keep hearing that I need to step into the real world? My life is the real world...it is MY real world!

Darkness is defined as the absence of light. Darkness isn't a place, it isn't a reality, but rather it is the result of a reality. The reality is that one can't seem to find or identify the light. The void is described as darkness. Therefore, there is only one sure way to escape the darkness–to walk into the light.

Darkness, sadness, blackness, evil...none of this is of God. Most of us have experienced darkness. From the inside out, from the outside in, we've been touched by darkness. We have either been exposed to the darkness or we have seen the effects of darkness in the lives of others. Darkness represents different places for each of us, but it tends to have the same destructive impact on all of our lives. I wonder if we are better off if the darkness in life is never exposed.

Sometimes I feel like my darkness really had less to do with hardships or tragedies than I thought at that time. I never quite felt fulfilled although I knew God was what could fill my life. Even still, I am grateful to God for his grace and favor upon me.

The darkness really set in after I had graduated from college, which was yet another miracle from God. Graduating from college was one of those dreams that I knew was possible, yet I also knew it would be difficult. Throughout my life, I believed that if I was good to people and was generally a good person, that my life would actually be filled with good things. How disillusioned is that? Because my young life had been pretty uneventful, this appeared to be the case. I had not experienced any major disruptions or disappointments so I didn't really know how I would deal with controversy or tribulation. It would still be years before I would understand the difference in living safe and being saved!

When I graduated from college in 1989, I had difficulty securing a job. I had a college degree, self-confidence, high morals and a good work ethic. So you can imagine how crushed I was to keep hearing "you don't have enough experience" during my job search. Because I got tired of hearing this response, I lowered my standards and my expectations. The response changed. I began to hear "your credentials are impressive, but you're overqualified." This feels incredibly like the real world to me—four years of college, tens of thousands of dollars in student loans and I can't find a job. Obviously "Mr. Bill" didn't realize that I had not found a job, because many of them kept coming in my mailbox. Whether there is money or not, bills are the absolute introduction to the real world. Even when I did finally start working, there was still never enough money. If my pay increased, my lifestyle would change, and the expenses and bills would increase. There is darkness in the struggle of never having enough. This was my reality. The struggle to work and not be appropriately compensated created a heavy, weary, feeling of drudgery–there was never a moment when I wasn't wondering how to stay afloat. But since I wasn't walking with God, I was wearing a steel ball that made dealing with this even more difficult.

The only bright spot in my life at that time was that I had found a really great apartment and had a wonderful roommate. She had been my best friend since third grade. But even this bright spot would not be bright enough to prepare me for what would come next in my life.

The phone call–4:00 in the morning–it's cold in Massachusetts in January. Am I dreaming or is the phone really ringing? I woke up and the ringing continued. The voice on the other end was not a familiar voice. It was an official sounding call, a male voice, but almost distant sounding. The call and the voice were both dreadful sounds. He asked if my mother was Deloris. Was Deloris? WAS Deloris? Hesitantly, I responded "yes."

Then, another question "Did she live at _____? DID she live at _____, WHY WAS THIS MAN TALKING TO ME IN PAST TENSE? Then the bomb dropped! "She has passed away at home, in her sleep, and we need you to come and identify the body before we can move her.". WHAT IS THIS? He spoke as if he was talking about an animal that he found beside the road. I guess this is how he handled the duties of his job. His routine of notifying the family was probably annoying to him, especially in the early morning hours. This was not routine nor was it normal to me, so I was silent as I gathered myself and tried to understand what I had just heard. I couldn't breathe! There was no air in the room! I couldn't feel my legs! Where was I! I was completely numb. Perhaps this really was a dream. I needed to wake up, that's it. But again, I realized that I was already awake. This is not happening. My mom is young, so he is obviously making a mistake. My mom is only 42. So, I don't get this. There is nothing about this that makes sense to me.

Even after I accepted the notion that I was obviously not sleeping, this would prove to be the darkest moment I would ever live through. Darkness—and my life was not even close to seeing any daylight.

My first task was to notify my brother. This would be devastating to him; after all, my mother is his best friend. He had always been so much closer to her than I had been. As much as I loved and admired her, in the midst of my grief, my heart was heavy for him. For some reason, I believed that his loss would be greater than mine. So we spoke for a moment and decided that we would go to my mother's house and handle this together. After speaking to my brother, I went into the bedroom of my apartment mate and all I could say was "she's dead". It had not felt real until that moment when I spoke it.

It was in that moment that my soul drifted away. It was also in that moment that a part of me died. Everything I thought was possible in my future seemed to die with the loss of my mother. I didn't know where I would find the strength to move forward. Although she had taught me so much, there is nothing that I could pull from that would have prepared me for this. I had lived a life that was mostly positive, confident, and lively, but that had now all drifted away. My dreams, my life, my hopes, everything about who I had become or what I hoped to be had all drifted away. The only thing left was a cold, huge, open space, a dark place…this darkness that would overtake me for years to come. I would live in this darkness for far too many years of my life.

I don't recall what happened next. Did I take a shower? I don't know. There was water on my face. But was it from the shower or had I been crying? I don't know! God lifted me up enough to do what I had to do next. I don't recall the ride or how I even got out of the room. But I felt the weakness in my legs when I walked into the bedroom where my mother's lifeless body lay. What I remember most about that moment was the look on my mother's face. I remember the uncanny, but pleasant and peaceful smile. Something within me rose up and I quietly began to praise God. The look on my mother's face was one of peace as she transitioned to her new life. A tear of gladness made its way down my cheek. I stood there, looking at her beautiful face. It seemed like an eternity. She looked so peaceful; I thought that perhaps she was sleeping. So I stood there, looking, almost waiting for her to open her eyes. But her eyelids never parted. The peaceful silence was interrupted by the sound of the coroner saying, "I need one of you to help me move her." Up to this point, I felt that I had been floating in the air looking down at her face. But with the sound of the coroner's voice, I fell to the floor with a boom, and back to this reality. When my mind caught up with what was happening, that feeling returned and once again I could not breathe. The room started spinning and I just had to get out of there. I was light headed and felt that I was mere seconds from falling over. The spinning didn't stop, so now everything in the room looked as though I was looking through fog. But now, I had no tears. I supposed that even they were unsure of how to handle this moment. When we are young, it seems meaningless to hear someone say how important it is to love your mother because you only get one. There was nothing that ever seemed more like wisdom realized too late at that moment than that statement.

I thought I was well prepared to handle life. But in one unforeseen night…a heart attack, in her sleep, my mother…. I wasn't prepared for this. My life was gone and what little might have been left over would become a pit of despair. I would dwell in this place for over eight long years beyond this day. Today, I have come to the realization that it is destructive to allow oneself to slip so deep into darkness. I now realize how close I was to giving up. But what has also become apparent to me was that the deeper I allowed myself to fall into this pit, the more difficult it would be to pull myself out.

My brother and I arranged to have my mother flown to North Carolina to be laid to rest. This unforgettable date of January 10, 1992 still remains the single most devastating day in my life. The only thing that calmed my spirit during that time was a verse in Isaiah 41:10: "Fear thou not for I am with thee, be not dismayed for I am thy God, I will strengthen thee; yea I will help thee; yea I will uphold thee with the right hand of my righteousness."

Perhaps this is why in 1993 when my job announced that it was closing, it wasn't quite as devastating. At 25 years of age, I had lost the two things in life that most people feel they can't live without—my mom and my job. I felt that I needed a change of scenery. So I made the life-changing decision to move to Jacksonville, Florida and accept a job there. I don't remember living anyplace but in Massachusetts for much of my life, so I had no idea what to expect in Florida. Would I be able to take the heat? How long would it take to make friends? Where would I live?

None of this was significant right, because all I knew was I had to get away from the pain. I associated this pain with the only place I had ever known.

I ran away from the pain, or so I thought. Why had I not figured out that the pain would follow me? Why had I dismissed the possibility that the memories of the past would always be memories of the past? Why was it hard to accept that the memory of the person who meant the most in the world to me would not fade simply by putting miles between me and the incident?

This was a vivid and dark time in my life and I believe that sharing it is therapeutic for me; so I hope it will provide healing for someone else. For no matter how deep the darkness or how large the cloud, no matter how long it was going to take to get out of that place, I held onto the glimmer of hope for a brighter day.

There is a way out of the darkness, but the only way is through Christ. The only thing that can change Darkness is The Light! He was the only one who could bring me out of the level of despair that had so greatly consumed me. Through this period, I realized that if I stretched my arms high enough to try to reach for Him that His arms were long enough to reach me, wherever I was! I praise God for reaching down and pulling me up out of this place and not allowing me to die in the darkness. Finally, I know with complete certainty that there is no place so deep or dark that He can't reach.

Also, I am certain that there will be future struggles and I know that I will fall again, but I am certain that God will not allow me to stay there. The other lesson I learned during this process was that the goal of the enemy was to keep me in a place of despair. My pain was his pleasure.

Upon my revival from the depths of darkness, I realized that I had tucked away every thought of the things that the Lord had given me to be grateful for. The reality is that this didn't begin that night in my mother's apartment. I had been in a state of depression for many years. Part of my healing was accepting that I had lived much of my life not knowing what it was to be happy. This was primarily because I didn't know what joy or true happiness looked like. I was stuck in a hole of not enough. I was never satisfied; felt I didn't have enough and that I was never enough, therefore I was never at peace with who I was. But God and the mighty power of His grace...rescued me!

As I reflected on what I was feeling during that time, I realized that the darkness that had engulfed me had not begun with the loss of my mother. Although it's not uncommon for this type of grief to cause people to fall into a deep, dark place, I was in a deep sleep long before the grief was introduced in my life. But I realized that I had to wake up or I feared I would sleep forever. The ultimate plan of the enemy was to cause me to stay down. It was at this time when I found myself at one of the most important crossroads in my life. I would either drop even deeper in the Abyss, lost in the dark depths with no return, or I would allow a miracle to take place in my life and I would rise back up to where God was calling me to be. I chose to swim from the murky depths where I had sunk to ascend to a place far from the darkness. The hand of God guided me.

Most people may not understand what it is to be dead on the inside while displaying a smile on the outside, no matter how false and intermittent it actually was. For over eight years I had managed to wearily trudge forward. As I began to move *out of this place, I spent some time thinking upon how I got there and why I had stayed for so long.*

As is true with so many people, we sometimes look for help in all the wrong places. Although, there were people who genuinely tried to help me through this time, there were also people who were sent by the enemy to use my weakness as a way of keeping me from pursuing the Light.

One day in the spring of 1999 as I was visiting a local park, I was drawn to a young man sitting in the park with a book. He was reading the Bible, and his countenance lured me closer with such a strong desire that I had to talk to him. He said to me that he was a Prophet of Revelations and that he gave warnings to people who needed to be saved. He said that time was crucial. We debated back and forth about my personality, my good nature and my giving spirit and my demeanor. I continued to sell myself to him. I assured him of my good nature and told him what a good person I am and how I am always good to others. I told him that I love God and I know that God loves me. However, I was blown away when he looked at me and said, "That isn't enough!" So he asked me if I love God as I say I love God, then why had I not given my life to Him. I didn't know the answer to that question. There was no reason. We talked that day for nearly four hours in the park. And although I heard his message, I was not ready to heed his warning. So he finally asked me, "When will you ask Jesus to be your Lord and Savior?" My response was, "I will... One day, when I feel more ready." He said with almost a sense of urgency, "You could wait and one day might be too late." He finished with asking me, what it would take for me to "get it"?

Either it was irony or there were things being presented in my life to help me "get it." But several things happened shortly thereafter. Later that month, I was scheduled to receive results from a biopsy to test lumps in my throat. Obviously my greatest fear was that they would be cancerous. So is this going to be plight…my mother's death, loss of job, and now the possibility of cancer? As soon as I rose up from one event, another life-changing event occurred.

Here we go again….

One day as I was walking to my car, I was attacked and robbed at gunpoint. It's not difficult to guess what came next. It was this event that would make me "get it." This was the game changer that caused me to realize that I had to ask Jesus to be my Lord and Savior.

So that night I found myself on my knees. I cried, I prayed, I cried louder, I prayed louder. I confessed my sins, I thanked Jesus for dying for my sins and then I asked Him into my life. When I got up off the floor, I was exhausted, to the Lord cradled me to sleep.

When I awoke the next morning, I knew without a shadow of a doubt that something was different. I had a renewed enthusiasm for life. I had awakened in this same one bedroom apartment for several years now, but today, it felt like a different place. The dingy walls suddenly looked brighter. The things that appeared blurred just the night before suddenly seemed crystal clear. Even the plants in the apartment looked over watered on most days, and appeared to lack water on other days. But today, they looked green and vibrant…as if someone had brought them back to life while I was asleep.Wait a minute…is this me… smiling…?

Is this me, with a childish giggle?

I felt young and free, and for the first time in months, looked out of my window and saw the sun shining brightly.

The love of God was so newly present in my existence that it had broken through the darkness and had pulled me out! It had pulled me out just in time! The pain that my heart had felt for so many years—that pain that had become my normal, was non-existent.

I could not believe this miracle that I was witnessing and that I was feeling. I almost could not believe that I was the same person who woke up in this apartment just 24 hours prior with a different life and a different outlook than I now felt.

I was overwhelmed–to the degree that I sank to my knees and praised God. I had to thank Him for His Saving Grace!

He had delivered me out of the darkness which had surrounded my being. And He shined His light in the deep places of my life. The light that I felt had suddenly been turned on in my apartment was actually the light that had been turned on inside of me!

So this is the rebirth, the new life, the new creation–so this is what I had heard about!

It was real!

My former self had died and a new me had been born!
It was a new day and I was packing the peace and love that can only come from Jesus.

Jesus is a white light
Shrow(u)ded in God's Mighty Light

Chapter 6

"When thou passest through the waters, I {will be} with thee; and through the rivers, they shall not overflow thee: when thou walkest through the fire, thou shalt not be burned; neither shall the flame kindle upon thee."
Isaiah 43:2

Set Free

Set free from bondage—

A New Life in Jesus—

What does it really mean to be set free? Being free can be defined as no longer in slavery. Freedom is no longer under restraints or in oppression. Acknowledging one's freedom can be powerful and can be life altering. Sometimes the freedom is a state of mind, but most often when referenced from a spiritual perspective, it is freedom from the strongholds and the constant grips of the enemy. Freedom is the feeling of resting peacefully in the arms of the Father.

"He, whom the Son has set free, is free indeed."

John 8:36

There is no true freedom like the freedom that is found in Christ. Monti had spent so much of his adult life in bondage and mental anguish due to a grief that had consumed him. He didn't know how to free himself from that place of darkness, so Jesus stepped in and set him free. This chapter in Monti's writings gives me a warm and peaceful feeling. When he wrote of being set free, I knew that he had found his place in Jesus.

I've been set free from bondage…A bondage within myself.

Everything that had occurred in my past was where it should be—in the past!

Along with my new life, I began to have a new way of thinking. I hoped that this feeling would last forever. I really didn't know what to expect if the "newness" of salvation would be temporary or if this feeling would last always. Well, I realized that it doesn't just last effortlessly, but it was part of the plan to help me complete my assignment in this new life. To keep growing in the Lord and to stay on track with the Lord's plan, I would be required to do some things. So living this new life has its privileges but it also has its requirements. I knew that I would have to gain greater knowledge and insight in this new relationship in order to understand what would be expected of me.

Once I took that step to seek God to change my life, my perspective of life changed as well as my perception of who He was in my life. My life took on a whole new look. The pain and anguish I had felt for those years since my mother's death had finally subsided. There was a peace that surpassed my understanding and a comfort that I knew had to come from God.

With this new outlook on life, there were many things that I could see much clearer than ever before. I thought about all the times I had looked for love, thinking I would find the answer to my despair. The lesson I took from that experience was that I was searching for something external to relieve an internal pain. When I realized that the love that had been absent from my life was the love which comes from God, I was free to receive that which He promises to all of His children. There is a love that I must have for others and the love that I must have for myself. When I realized this, my eyes were opened. My greatest concern became my love for God and my ability to love others sincerely.

In addition to learning how to love, another aspect to my newfound freedom in Him was my change in focus. I can't believe how much time I spent in my past worrying about what I didn't have and how little time I spent being grateful for what I did. With this new focus, my prayer life changed tremendously. I became more passionate about my spirituality and more focused on my relationship with Christ. I have to admit that I would not have made it mentally, physically, or spiritually had this change in my prayer life not occurred.

I was reminded that only God knows the desires of my heart, therefore I had to pray fervently that He would search my heart and know how much I desired to be free of the pain and anguish I felt over my mother's passing. Only He could have healed that wound. Now that I have found peace regarding this huge loss, I can view death differently.

During my cancer scare, it is prayer that got me through without losing my mind…my prayers, the prayers of my church, the prayers of my friends, and the intense prayers of my family, mainly my Aunt Trish and her prayer groups or everyone she could bring on board…the clean bill of health and negative test results were simply because of prayer.

Nobody can tell me that there is not power in prayer.

For nearly three months after I was freed from bondage, I floated on this cloud called salvation that brought love, peace and comfort as I had never felt before. Sleep was better than it had ever been, the sun shone brighter than it ever had, and my prayer time with God became the highlight of my day. All I wanted was for everyone to feel what I was feeling, so I prayed for everybody!

I have always loved the beach. I love the sight and the smell of water. I've always felt God's presence when I'm near the water. I feel like he can hear me so much more clearly when I pray at the water. God's wonderful and majestic bodies of water stretching out as far as the eye can see and then touching the horizon off in the distance are so powerful and immense. Water is such a mysterious force of nature. Yet, even my awe at the sight of the ocean becomes miniscule when I think of the power of God. My understanding of his power overwhelms yet humbles me. Victory in my life and over all of life's circumstances now belonged to God.

CHAPTER 7

> *"Blessed {be} God, even the Father of our Lord Jesus Christ, the Father of mercies, and the God of all comfort; (4) Who comforteth us in all our tribulation, that we may be able to comfort them which are in any trouble, by the comfort wherewith we ourselves are comforted of God." II Corinthians 1: 3–4*

A NEW LIFE

During the final year of Monti's life, I saw the handsome, young man that I knew and loved all of his life; grow weak in spirit and in body. As I saw my nephew falling deeper into a place that I thought might be a place of no return, I prayed with him and for him often. It was at this time that I loaned him the book *You Have to Face it to Fix it* by William Watley. I never received the book back until we were clearing his home following his death. As I flipped the pages of the book, I noticed that he had written on several pages within several chapters.

In addition, there was a long message on the back inside cover. These are his written words:

"Trish, I love God, I love all people. Loving me was the hardest part. Thus I lacked confidence—just like Peter, I didn't

like myself as much as I should. I have looked closely at myself, under the conviction of the word of the Lord, and now being in conversion, becoming a completely different person, the word of the Lord is comfort. I realize God made me, and loves me, and believes in me, and if I want to be like Him, I must do the same. I love myself…(You always knew I'd get there). Father God (Lord Jesus) Please return blessings and favor to this child of yours that does your great works and whom you use and have helped me so. In Jesus name I pray. With a sincere heart and pure love (By God), I love you Aunt Trish and my sister in Christ—thanks for letting the Lord use you to enlighten me—it has moved my spirit and I have grown tremendously. Thank you Lord, Thank you, Aunt Trish. Again, sorry for writing all up in your book, but I was so compelled to do so. Love to Live, Live to Love. I pray and will strive to stay focused on the Lord, maintain and grow in Him forevermore. In Jesus name I pray, Amen."

When I read this, I was reminded of the many nights that I spent sitting on the bathroom floor in my house on the phone, as my husband slept upstairs…praying with Monti for hours. I remember trying so hard sometimes to encourage him when he was living in Florida…but I would feel that the more I prayed, the deeper he would sink. Sometimes we would talk on the phone for four or five hours, until he came back "up," and then we would just speak of the goodness of God. He always thought I was much stronger than I actually was. I would sometimes just cry because I felt his pain, I felt his loneliness; I felt the brokenness in his heart that had not mended following my sister's death.

For much of his adult life, I felt the need to pray much for his covering and his protection. He always seemed so fragile, but he was so much stronger than I gave him credit for.

What amazes me is how someone can have so many people who care about them, yet feel so alone when they are going through the trials of life. I have wondered what it must have felt like to feel empty inside and not be able to fill that void. That was the place deep inside of Monti.

But, I also remember the excitement when he realized that he would be able to move back to North Carolina. God's plan is always so awesome and so timely. Only God could have known the number of Monti's days and only He could have orchestrated it such that those final years were spent with the people who loved him most. He drew closer to his grandmother than he ever had before. He was able to attend family functions; he had missed so many of them for so many years. And I'm glad to have spent time watching him laugh.

He spent a fair amount of time at my house and he spent time visiting each of his aunts. I remember him staying with my son while my husband and I went on an anniversary trip. He said that he liked it there because there was peace. He drew a picture of God sitting on the throne which he said he saw every time he sat at the top of the stairs and watched the sun shine through the front window. He drew several pictures during that visit.

I am grateful that he felt peace and love there.

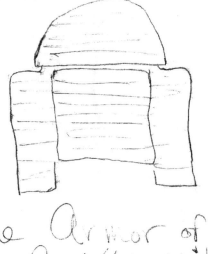

A Gift
The Armor of God for Protection–A Promise
(Golden like "The Throne")
Reinforced–There are cracks–be careful-be prayerful
Faith is the Armor–Trust in Him

CHAPTER 8

"Yea, though I walk through the valley of the shadow of death, I will fear no evil: for thou {art} with me; thy rod and thy staff they comfort me." Psalm 23:4

THE END OR HIS BEGINNING

The last months and weeks of Monti's life were difficult. During his stay in the hospital, I would leave work every day and go sit with him. I would call him several times throughout the day to see how he was feeling and every day, we prayed. Every day, I was more and more encouraged. For some reason, there was something about this time in the hospital that made me think that he would be getting better very soon. As it got closer to the time that I thought he would be released, I began to suspect that his illness was not something that he would easily overcome.

I remember one visit in particular. The doctor came in the room and I proceeded to leave. For the first time, Monti told me to stay and hear what the doctor was telling him. I could see that he didn't have much energy and I knew that he was weak. I had seen him weak before, but what the doctor spoke during that visit was something I was not prepared to hear. I remember his words, sounding so matter of fact…"Because he is HIV positive, he will need to take medication for the rest of his life." I tried to show no emotion, no change of expression because he and Monti both proceeded as though this was not the first time I should have heard this. Have you ever known something to be true deep down in your spirit, but you felt that if you didn't speak it, you didn't have to accept it to be true? That was my moment. I may have mentioned that visit to my husband and perhaps one of my sisters. But we already knew. We just didn't talk about it. We couldn't talk about it. My mother wasn't at a place to receive that, so we didn't say it, which made it not so.

I don't remember which hospital stay it was, but many days that I went to visit Monti, he would rest. But when he wasn't resting, we laughed and talked. My nephew was one of the funniest people I knew. He could find the humor in everything. His whole face would laugh when he said something funny! When we weren't laughing, we talked. He talked about Florida, he talked about his writing, he talked about our time in Massachusetts, he talked a lot about his brother, Joe, but most of the time, he talked about his mom. And though he knew the necessity of it, he spoke often of not wanting to take all of that medication. That day the doctor told me how long they thought he could live with the medication or if he chose not to take medication. Since the "with medication" time-frame was in the distant future, I don't think I allowed myself to hear the rest of the prognosis. My mind never comprehended the "without medication" information. I assumed he would take it so anything else was irrelevant.

During one visit, I bought him a book explaining the 23rd Psalm. Sometimes, I read pages from the book because I thought that it would encourage him. If not, it would at least encourage me.

Even though it was becoming increasingly more obvious that he was extremely sick, I still hadn't accepted how sick he was. Even after he left the hospital, I don't think I realized how sick he was until the hospice bed appeared in his living room. I remember hearing something that sounded so much like "maybe only six months to live!" Why is that statement such a haze in my memory? Where did that come from? Did that mean that he had stopped taking the medicine? Apparently so, because by all indications; he was sick, now, for real.

It was Sunday. Everyone had gone to church. My sister phoned and said she thought that all of us should come over to see Monti, he was pretty sick. By this time, his brother Joe had moved to North Carolina to stay with him and take care of him "until he got better."

My sisters and I went to his apartment. He lay across the hospice bed, then he sat up on the bed, he coughed a lot, he tried to laugh some—but what I remember most is how he looked that day. He was a fragment of the man I loved like my own son. I remember my sister crying because of how thin he had gotten. My heart was broken. I just wanted to make sure that he knew how much we all loved him and how deeply we cared for him.

We all talked about him not taking his medication. But again, he spoke of how it made him feel. It was also quite obvious that he was not eating properly. We left the apartment for a while to shop for foods that would be easy for him to digest and would hopefully help him get his strength back.

We brought back chicken broth, gelatin, ginger ale… We filled his cabinets with things that we thought he would eat…but in just a few short days, he would be gone.

Immediately after Monti's passing, we cleaned out his apartment. I saved his writings because I was determined that one day his silenced voice would be heard. As we cleared his belongings from the apartment, there were some things about his life that became clearer to me. I was able to better understand his lifestyle and life choices. As we looked around, we could see the things that he cherished most. With this new revelation, I better understood his life; however, there were many unanswered questions about his death.

What is congenital heart failure and what caused it? He was too young for this.

Could this be what the doctor was saying that day in the hospital that I had blocked out?

Had he really stopped taking his medicine?

Maybe he had heart problems and no one knew? After all, his mom died with heart problems.

Had he told anyone what the doctor said about his illness?

He had survived so much–his cancer scare, the attack. He had suffered so much loss, grief and pain...had he decided that he would no longer continue to fight?

Did he lose hope or was his hope now in seeing whom he loved most?

The two things that Monti had loved most in his life occupied his being. I believe that as he grew weaker and as he got sicker, his desire to see Jesus and to see his mom became greater than the desire to carry on. I believe that the medicine and the medical care to attempt to prolong his life simply became the obstacles that kept him away from where he desired to be.

Perhaps he felt justified in not taking his medication and not taking care of himself. Could it be that he had a plan to see the two people whom he felt loved him his whole life; the two people who accepted him, no matter what he was dealing with; the two people who comforted him when he was alone; the two people who understood him when no one else did? Could it be that the spirits of the two people who he desired most to see obviously summoned him to join them?

It seems that's exactly what he did.

CHAPTER 9

"For we have not an high priest which cannot be touched with the feeling of our infirmities; but was in all points tempted like as {we are, yet} with- out sin. Let us therefore come boldly unto the throne of grace, that we may obtain mercy, and find grace to help in time of need." Hebrews 4: 15-16

THE LETTER

I found this letter in Monti's apartment; the writing is sloppy and incoherent. But it shares a moment when he slipped back into darkness for a little while.

Everybody, I don't know what else to do. I tried to get help. I was treated like I was wasting everybody's time at the emergency room. Had to have a suicide plan to get help. Want death all can think about, can't stop thinking how to get there. Don't want Hell. Maybe God will understand no other options left. I tried to get help. They turned me away into a worse storm–hurricane–knowing I couldn't yet help–turned me out into nowhere. No one can help me. God won't take me. Yet maybe I can take pain pills for pain and sleep–sleepin' means no thoughts; I pray I wake up with my Lord. The world (earth) is not my home. Nobody wants me, where do I belong. Even the emergency room turned on me. _____ said get back in to the church, wipe my eyes and be a man? I felt so weak and stupid. She's right but I don't know how to be better. Can't deal with people, no compassion. I am weak and therefore prey. I love only—hard to love myself. Tell Joe I'm sorry. I'm sorry I'm going back—don't know what will happen. Hopefully the hurricane will kill me on the way. Will be by nature that it happened. I hope God will take me and accept me. He knows all I've gone through and how hard it's been. Nothing left on earth—there's just Him. I pray I don't end up in Hell. The hospital has left me no choice. Have to have a plan to get help. I wish something could have been done before it got this far. Called EAP he said ER would help. They didn't. I was embarrassed and belittled. Help Me.

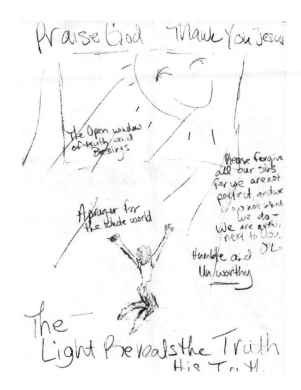

Praise God–Thank You Jesus
The Open window of truth and Blessings
A prayer for the whole world
Please forgive all our sins for we are not perfect, and we
know not what we We are nothing next to You, O Lord.
Humble and Unworthy
The Light Reveals the Truth–His Truth

Chapter 10

"Go, said Jesus, your faith has healed you." Mark 10:52

My Future *(with Jesus)*

As I write this very line, I hear Gospel music in the background. I hear and feel the music and its lyrics. It moves through me like energy. I can't get through one single day without thinking about all He has done for me and all He has brought me through. I'm giving praise to His Holy name. Why hadn't I trusted Him with everything? Because of Him I am. Not just my birth, but to still be alive now, and to wake to each day with a sound mind and healthy body. I have to say each and every morning… "Thank you Father for allowing me to wake to another day."

As I think about my future, I must think of the future of our entire existence, everyone's existence. I am merely a soldier in the army of the Lord.

In representing my Father up above, one of my greatest prayers is that how I feel about Him isn't just heard from my mouth, but rather witnessed by the light that shines from me. This light would represent evidence of the Lord's presence in me…and is a direct confirmation that He exists…and more than that, He exists in us. What a wonderful world it would be if I, as well as everyone in this world, was right where God wants us all to be, or at least working towards that goal. Since sin was born into the world, we all know that the ideal society cannot exist. But in this battle, I hope God's children realize there is only one Master that can be served. I pray they all, as I have, will choose God.

What the world needs is Love. And God is Love. The world needs more of God. There are many events, opinions, and facts that exist as revelations. The world and its people are more than just caught up in sin. It's quickly getting worse and worse. And still the battle rages on with so many people ignorant to how important it is to fight for what is right and what this means for our future. The future of this world, that is. There is no need for me to remind everyone of all the signs and disastrous things that are taking place all around us—all the suffering and pain. There is such a lack of humanity and compassion for one another. Where is the love? Where is the faith? Where is the loyalty– loyalty to the creator of everything?

I could never be ashamed or afraid to show or say how much I love the Lord. How could I not praise Him after all He's done for me, and what he has delivered me from? He has done the same for so many others. He can definitely do the same for you.

I do not want to appear to be shoving anything down anyone's throat. What I write here is a personal account of my life, beliefs, and value system. Everyone is entitled to have their own, and I will respect those choices. I have so much more to learn and experience. I know that many trials and struggles lie ahead. I will face them with a confidence in a victory over all *bad things and evil that comes my way. I am at peace because I know that God is the Alpha and the Omega, the beginning and the end. Creator, Forgiver, Father, Comforter, Reliever of all pain, Giver of mercy and of love, and Deserver of my praise. So my life is dedicated to Him.*

I thank you,
Monti

MONTI FITZGERALD FINNIE

December 27, 1967–September 28, 2004

"Love to Live, Live to Love."

Souls in danger, look above, Jesus completely saves,
He will lift you by His love, out of the angry waves.
He's the Master of the sea, billows His will obey,
He your Savior wants to be, be saved today.
Love lifted me, Love lifted me,
When nothing else would help
Love lifted me!

THE END

"But ye are a chosen generation, a royal priesthood, an holy nation, a peculiar people; that ye should shew forth the praises of him who hath called you out of darkness into his marvelous light." I Peter 2:9

WORKING THROUGH THE DARKNESS TO THE LIGHT

SELF REFLECTION

Monti's despair was magnified because of unresolved grief from loss as a result of death. Many of us face loss on a regular basis. We experience loss of loved ones, loss of jobs, loss of relationships–and in all of it, we are changed.

Many times we fail to establish our new life absent of what we have lost. Therefore, we have a hole in our existence that we attempt to fill with all of the wrong things.

In reading *Monti's Story* I hope that you found joy in knowing that through his grief and depression, he knew Christ and he knew the love of Christ in his life. I believe that his desire for the fullness of the light overpowered the darkness from his loss even though he had not emotionally and physiologically dealt with the grief associated with his mother's death.

Now that you have read through the story, I hope that you will use this time to think back on Monti's life and use it as a resource to determine if you or if someone you love might need to work through the process of finding the light in the midst of a dark place.

The following questions are to generate a thought process to help you determine if you need to seek further help in developing a new normal in your revised state of being.

What loss have you experienced recently?

_____

_____

_____

_____

_____

Is there someone close to you to discuss this loss with? If so, are you comfortable that they can listen without judging and can provide Godly counsel or can provide guidance to seek the counsel needed?

_____

_____

_____

_____

_____

What has been the most difficult thing to deal with since the loss?

_____

_____

_____

_____

_____

Has this loss impacted your decision making ability?

_____

_____

_____

_____

_____

Has your mental or physical health changed since this loss?

_____

_____

_____

_____

_____

Use the following space to write out what you are feeling as a result of this loss. Be specific regarding your feelings and your emotions.

> *"Therefore the redeemed of the Lord shall return, and come with singing unto Zion; and everlasting joy {shall be} upon their head: they shall obtain gladness and joy; {and} sorrow and mourning shall flee away." Isaiah 51:11*

_____

_____

_____

_____

_____

_____

_____

_____

_____

_____

_____

_____

_____

_____

NOW TAKE A MOMENT TO TALK ABOUT IT TO GOD…

Dear God,

Thank you for sustaining me in the midst of my loss. Thank you for loving me when love has felt scarce in my life. Thank you for family and friends who have and who will support me through this time.

I am seeking your light in the dark places of my life. Because I know that you are a healer, I am seeking you for healing over every area of my life.

With each day, let me feel the hurt less and less, and let me feel your presence more and more.

I give the pain to you.
I give the despair to you.
I give the depression to you.

And now I am made new in you.

Amen

FINAL THOUGHT:

Seek God regarding where you might be able to receive wise and compassionate counseling. Don't go through your storm alone. God Bless You!

Rev. Trish